Good Day or Bad Day
I Love You Anyway!

By Sigal Adler

Illustrated By Pixel Ink Studio

One day, the monster woke up with a pout,
"Wake up, sleepy!" his mother called out.
"I won't ask you again," his mother said.
He finally managed to roll out of his bed.

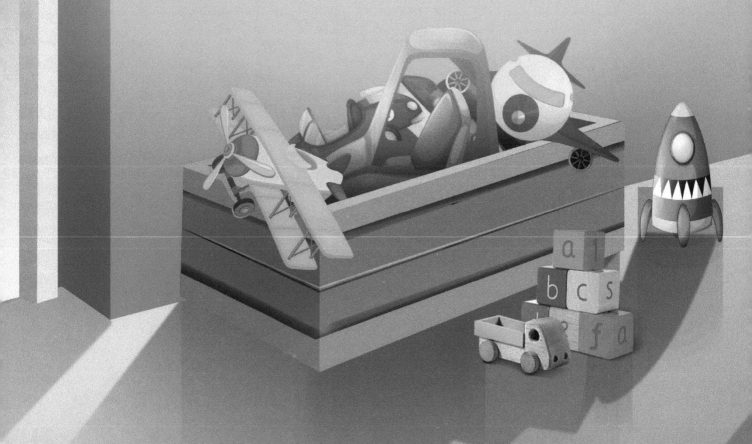

The monster started his day on the wrong foot,
it was quite unpleasant and made him off-put.
Nothing worked out, it was all quite a mess,
"What a terrible day!" he said in distress.

The poor little thing, woke up very upset,
thinking: "how much worse can it get?"
But mom was in a hurry, and made it clear:
"We have to go now, there's no time, my dear."

That morning, mom had to say everything twice:
"Please brush your teeth and wear something nice.
Where are your shoes, you're not ready at all...?
Why did you pour so much milk in that bowl?"

Of course, the monster got milk on his shirt,
but luckily mom could handle any kind of dirt.
"Here's a clean one," his loving mom said,
"I can't be late for work," she asked and pled.

He somehow made it on time for class,
but even later at home, he spoke with sass.
"Those look gross" he pointed at his beans,
he wanted candy and refused to eat greens.

He made a mess and threw things around,
he dropped all his toys straight to the ground.
He kicked a ball, and then they heard a 'crash',
Mom's favorite vase came down with a smash.

Mom scolded him, "why can't you behave?
You're acting as wild as a troll from a cave.
Just do your homework, relax and sit down!"
But the little monster just gave her a frown.

Mom tried not to get angry, she did her best,
but she was very tired, had no second to rest.
Her son just would not take a shower,
convincing him, took her more than an hour

When the monster was dressed and dry,
he was happy to wave this day goodbye.
Having a bad day can be a real pain,
he hoped this wouldn't happen again.

He suddenly saw his mom on the couch,
and felt terribly sad for being a grouch.
The grouchy monster was wild and impolite,
he was rude to his mom and that wasn't right.

The little guy who had a rough day
hugged his mom and started to say:
"I'm sorry for today, I know it was wrong,
but this day was awful and so very long!"

He wanted to tell her why things went bad,
sometimes he's happy, and sometimes he's sad.
Sometimes he's strong, and at times he felt weak,
He liked to be quiet, but he also liked to speak.

Then he tried to explain, to tell her some more,
and was worried she loved him less than before.
He looked at his mom who seemed very tired,
"Do you want another kid?" he sadly inquired.

"Never!" Mom said and gave him a big hug,
"You're my son, my sweet little bug."
And then she asked: "and how about you?
Would you want another mom, too?"

"Not ever!" he said, with tears in his eyes,
"You should get 'the best mommy prize'.
And though we can argue, from morning till noon,
I love you so much, from here to the moon!"

That day indeed had started rather lousy,
but now he was pleased and getting drowsy.
Little monsters can have messy days, too,
but he should clean up, there was a lot to do.

It was night time and he was happily in bed,
his mom tucked him in and kissed his forehead.
She read him a book, they counted some sheep,
until he shut his eyes and fell deep asleep.

So, even though things didn't go well,
and both mom and son started to yell...
In the end, when all was said and done,
their fight was over and love had won.

After all, it could happen to anyone,
not all days can be pleasant and fun.
Monsters and people can feel down and sad,
but luckily most days, we're cheery and glad.

CPSIA information can be obtained
at www.ICGtesting.com
Printed in the USA
LVHW071334160621
690386LV00006B/151

9 781947 417472